YOU
COME
TOO !

Have fun

v2/95

"From noon till night they let things go,
In sky above and on earth below."

THE
ROOSEVELT BEARS
GO TO
WASHINGTON

By SEYMOUR EATON

(PAUL PIPER)

ILLUSTRATIONS BY
R. K. CULVER

DOVER PUBLICATIONS, INC.
NEW YORK

Published in Canada by General Publishing Company, Ltd., 30 Lesmill Road, Don Mills, Toronto, Ontario.

Published in the United Kingdom by Constable and Company, Ltd, 10 Orange Street, London WC2H 7EG.

This Dover edition, first published in 1981, is an unabridged republication of the work originally published in 1907 by Edward Stern & Company, Inc., Philadelphia, under the title "More About Teddy B. and Teddy G. The Roosevelt Bears Being Volume Two Depicting their further Travels and Adventures." The original color illustrations are reproduced here in black and white.

International Standard Book Number: 0-486-24163-7
Library of Congress Catalog Card Number: 81-66492

Manufactured in the United States of America
Dover Publications, Inc.
180 Varick Street
New York, N.Y. 10014

MORE ABOUT THESE BEARS

When in the autumn of 1905, I created the characters of TEDDY-B and TEDDY-G I builded better than I knew. I brought these bears out of their mountain den in Colorado and started them on their tour of the East to teach children that animals, even bears, may have some measure of human feeling; that the primary purpose of animals is not necessarily that of supplying sport for the hunter. That this lesson has been abundantly taught is proven by the overwhelming welcome given the Teddy Bears by the boys and girls of the United States; and it is safe to say that the traditional "bear will get you" has now and forever lost its frightening significance.

This book is a sequel to "The Travels and Adventures of the Roosevelt Bears," and completes the story of the tour of TEDDY-B and TEDDY-G from Colorado to Washington. The third volume will report in jingle and picture the tour of the Teddy Bears abroad.

Seymour Eaton

ATH-DARA
Lansdowne, Pa.

CONTENTS

LIST OF ILLUSTRATIONS

How The Roosevelt Bears reached NEW YORK

How The Roosevelt Bears reached NEW YORK

The Roosevelt Bears were born out West
In a big ravine near a mountain crest,
Where they lived as cubs and had such play
As Teddy Bears have every day.
But they learned some things as years went by
Of cities great and buildings high,
And trains that run at rapid speed,
And schools which teach folks how to read,
And circus clowns and phonograph
And other things which make folks laugh,
  And big hotels where meals they say
    Are served in style both night and day.
      They had heard of men of great renown
        Who lived and died in Boston town;
          Of rulers brave and statesmen bold
            And millionaires with barrels of gold;
              Of men who work just day by day
                For boys and girls and daily pay;
                  And of one they heard who works for fun:
                    The President at Washington.

These bears some travel books had found
Which told them the world is round.
They made up their minds that they would see
And learn about geography
And visit cities everywhere
And introduce the Teddy Bear.
They found some gold in a cave one day
Which they could use to pay their way.

"They found some gold in a cave one day."

So one bright morn they said good-bye
To cave and creek and mountain high,
To an old bobcat with a bandaged knee,
To a young cougar and squirrels three,
To a big-horn sheep and a mountain deer,
And to other friends that lived quite near;
And with bags on backs and sticks in hand
They started their tramp across the land.

The black bear's name was TEDDY–B;
    The B for black or brown, you see.

      And TEDDY–G was the gray bear's name;
          The G for gray; but both bears came
                For "Teddy" because everywheres
                Children called them Teddy Bears.

                The "Teddy" part is a name they
                  found
                On hat and tree and leggings round,
                On belt and boot and plates of tin,
                And scraps of paper and biscuits thin,
                And other things a
                  hunter dropped
                At a mountain
                  camp where he
                  had stopped.

The story tells how these Teddy Bears
Scattered forever all blues and cares,
And made fun and frolic and mischief too,
And did some tricks for bears quite new;

And how some boys, the stories tell,
Liked these two Teddy Bears so well
That they made a million for the stores to sell:
Some quite little, for children small,
And some as big as the bears are tall;

The brown ones looking like TEDDY–B,
And the white as funny as TEDDY–G.

"With bags on backs and sticks in hand,
They started their tramp across the land."

The story goes on to tell how far
These two bears rode in a Pullman car,
And the tricks they played on folks that night
When the colored porter put out the light;

And how TEDDY–G wouldn't sleep upstairs
"On a shelf," he said, "too small for bears."
He wanted a window; he wanted to see;
And he kept folks awake till half-past three.

And the story tells of other tricks
In the dining car, and of a mix
When TEDDY–G pulled a rope on top
And brought the train to a sudden
        stop;

And how the two were put off the
        train
On a Kansas farm in a shower of rain.
The fun they had from that time on
Fills every page of Book Number One.

They started by learning the
        famous trick
How farmer boys get ahead so
        quick.

But the things they did would
        take your breath,
For they scared the farmer half
        to death.

The horses were put at gathering eggs,
    And pigs walked round on two hind legs,
        And sheep were given the corn to hoe
            And potatoes to plant and wheat to sow.

The story tells how an angry bull
Made a pasture field look pretty full
And chased the two bears round a stack
And over the top and down and back.

From there to a district school they went,
On mischief and education bent,
Where things were done by TEDDY–B,
Who hit the desk and said that he

Would make letters dance and figures fly
And good boys laugh and bad boys cry;
The questions he gave; and the boys,
    their look;
They had never seen them in a book:

If a camel can go without water a week
How long can he go if he owns a creek?
And this, to bound the moon and sky,
And name the capital of by-and-by;

    And a hundred more as hard and
        tough,
    Till the children said they had
        enough;
    But when they left the school that
        day
    The children were happy, the
        farmers say.

The story tells how in railway style
    They ran an engine for a mile
        And spent a day at a county show
        And helped the boys to make things go;
            How they walked on ropes drawn good and tight
            And jumped through hoops and landed right;

        And of the ride in an old balloon
        Which took them half-way to the moon;
        And things that happened in the sky that
           night
        And the way the world went out of sight;
        And how they landed in Lincoln Park
        In Chicago town
           just 'fore dark,

And the big hotel on a busy street
Where waiters brought them things to eat.
How they rang for bell-boys, just for fun,
    To give them a quarter and see them run;
      And the fun they made in vaudeville;
      Children are laughing about it still.

        And the bargain sale; TEDDY–G got
           lost;
        And the things they bought and what
           they cost;
        And their trip to Niagara Falls that night,
        And what they thought of Niagara's
           height,
        And the picnic boys and the boating stunt
        When they shot the rapids in a punt;
        And how the boys made cheering go
        When the train pulled out for Buffalo.

The story tells of their further jaunt
  And of TEDDY–G at a restaurant;
    How he missed his train and lost his mate;
    For TEDDY–B had risen late;
  And the jolly crowds the bears to greet
To cheer them all along the street

As they rode from station to Common green
In Boston town like king or queen;
And of the home on Beacon Hill
Where Priscilla Alden and her brother Will
Entertained them gladly days and nights
While they were seeing the Boston sights.

But the things they did in Boston town
Are done in picture and written down
In Volume One by Teddy's paw,
The jolliest book you ever saw.
It tells how they captured Bunker Hill
And worked like soldiers with stubborn will;
And how they got lost in Boston squares
Where criss-cross streets run everywheres;

And the time they had at Plymouth Rock
When trying to make forefathers talk;
And the auto ride to Lexington
Which nearly cost them all their fun,
For TEDDY–G would chauffeur be
And he ran that car like sixty-three;
It didn't run; he made it sail
And landed himself and his mate in jail.

The story tells of their Harvard tricks,
Where they got themselves in another
    mix
In getting degrees, a double-L-D,
Which didn't fit well on TEDDY–G;
It tells about the talking machine,
The funniest thing they had ever seen;

How they danced a two-step and sang as well
    And heard Uncle Josh his stories tell;
        It tells of the time when they went to see
            Where the Boston patriots made good tea
                In seventeen hundred and sixty-three;

And then of their sail in a little
    skiff,
And how a storm hit them a biff
And sent them out on the ocean
    wide,
Half-way across to the other side;
And how at noon there came in
    sight
A tower of ice all glistening white;

And how they met away out there
On this iceberg white a polar bear;
And the stories he told of a northern
    pole
Which was never seen by a living
    soul,
But it carried a flag both night and
    day,
The stars and stripes of the U. S. A.;

And the story tells of the rescue made
And how the steamer crowds hurrahed
As "Yankee Doodle" the brass band
    played;
And then it tells, this jolly book,
How reporters met them at Sandy Hook
And asked them questions and pictures
    took;
And of New York and its buildings high,
And how the bears made money fly,
And dressed in style to see the town,
To do Fifth Avenue up and down;

And the guide they hired, wee
    Muddy Pete,
A lad whose home was on the
    street,
And his little dog, a terrier white,
Pete's boon companion day and
    night.
The story tells of the circus show
Where the two bears helped to
    make things go;

How like heroes of a hundred fights
The Roosevelt Bears in colored tights
Stepped in the ring to dance or sing,
To ride or tumble or anything.

So these Teddy Bears are here to stay:
They came from the West one summer's
    day
And journeyed East from town to town
And gathered fame and much renown.

Book Number One (boys know it well)
    The pictures show and the stories tell
        Of how they crossed the U. S. A.
            (And made folks laugh both night and day)
            To New York City, there to be told
                That Teddy Bears in the shops were sold.
                    But the bears in the shops are only toys
                    Made to please good girls and boys.
                        These Roosevelt Bears, TEDDIES–B and G,
                        Are as full of mischief as you or me;
                        They laugh and talk and sleep and eat
                        And go around on two hind feet
                        And ride on cars and wear good clothes;
                    And the things they do, dear only knows,
                For they read from books and music play
                And lose themselves nearly every day.
            But the story here and these pictures new
        Tell things about them just as true
    As the things that happened, children say,
From West to East along the way.

The
Roosevelt Bears
put out a
FIRE

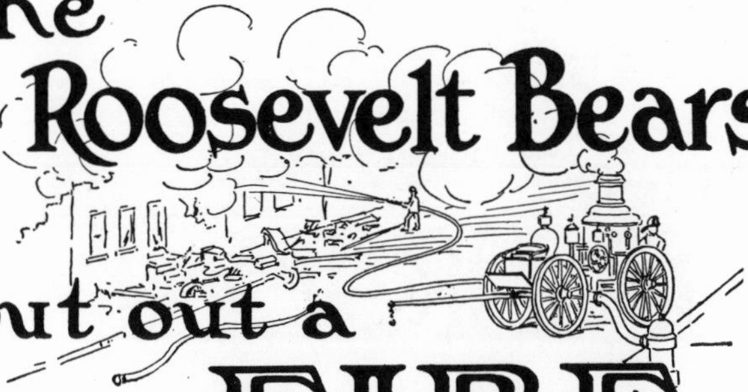

The Roosevelt Bears put out a FIRE

One day the Bears took trolley rides
With Muddy Pete and Cribs for guides.
The car was open; they enjoyed the air;
They helped the conductor collect the
    fare,

And pulled the bell to start or stop,
And fixed the trolley pole on top,
    And put on the brakes and rang the gong
    When teams in front didn't move along.

    But they got in trouble when TEDDY–G
Climbed on the roof of the car to see
The working of the electricity.

" But they got in trouble when TEDDY-G climbed on the roof of the car to see the working of the electricity."

"They climbed up ladders in clouds of smoke,
And lifted hose and windows broke."

What it was that hit him he didn't know,
But it hit so smart TEDDY–G let go
And tumbled off a dozen feet
From the trolley top down to the street.

The car was stopped; TEDDY–B got out
    To see what the trouble was all about;
    The conductor gave expert advice;
Muddy Pete replied with words not nice;
While Cribs stood round as if to say
"Let us try it again some other day."
"The thing that struck me," said TEDDY–G,
As he walked to the curb on hand and knee.

"Struck me all over, outside and in,
At every place like a prodding pin,
And burned like fire and did all so quick
I hadn't time to learn the trick."
       "Let the car go on," said TEDDY–B,
         "We'll stay right here this town to see
      And get some lunch and look around,
         And walk up that hill to that college ground,
And climb that pole on the public square
    And show the children playing there
      That the Roosevelt Bears have been to school
        And know A B C by rote and rule."

"You may go yourself,"
    said TEDDY-G,
"And see the town, but as
    for me,
I climbed one pole to-day
    before
And it left my bones a
    trifle sore.
I'll stay right here and rest a bit
The several places where I got hit."
While thus they talked Muddy Pete and
    Cribs
Went off to buy some roasted ribs
And fried potatoes and muffins hot
And three cups of coffee in a pot.

As they ate their lunch they heard a ring,
Both quick and loud: ding! ding! ding! ding!
    "A fire! fire!" cried Muddy Pete,
        And off the four ran down the street.
            TEDDY-G forgot about electricity
                And ran as fast as TEDDY-B.

They found the fire in a dry goods store
  And making its way towards three or four
    Of the largest shops on the busiest street:
      A clothing house and a store with meat,

And a great big grocery on the right
  And not a fireman yet in sight.
    The firemen's hall was across the street
      And in half a minute Captain Muddy Pete

Had told some boys that
  the job was theirs
And had given orders to
  the Roosevelt Bears

About the wagons and reel
  and hose,
And hooks and ladders and
  firemen's clothes.

Muddy Pete.

"I've seen a thousand fires," said he,
"And I know this thing from A to Z.
Slap on those togs: they fit you slick;
Boost out the reel; get busy quick;

Hitch up that rubber to that spouter there;
Twist round the stopper and let 'er tear.
Hang on to that nozzle, you TEDDY–G,
And point it straight at the fire you see.

"Up to a roof with hose in hand
And on the ridge to take his stand."

Now let 'er go!" and with swishing stroke
 The water struck the fire and smoke.
  In sixty seconds the Roosevelt team
   Were pouring water, a steady stream,
    On the blazing store and the crowd near by,
     Making women run, and children cry.

Captain Muddy Pete took full command
And told the Bears just where to stand,
And what to do and where to go,
And to point the nozzle high or low.

They climbed up ladders in clouds of smoke,
And lifted hose and windows broke,
And carried goods out to the street,
And burned their ears and scorched their feet.

They saved two boys from the highest floor
Who were in a room and had locked the door.
 The wind was blowing both hard and high,
 And it carried fire to roofs near by.

TEDDY–G.

TEDDY–G was ordered by Muddy Pete
 To carry a ladder across the street,
 And go up to a roof with hose in hand,
 And on the ridge to take his stand,

And turn the hose all round about
 Till every fire he could see was out.
 And thus they worked like trained firemen
 Till there wasn't a spark where the fires had
 been.

The man that owned the dry-goods store
Took the Bears to his home for an hour or
 more
And Cribs and Pete for cream and cake
And offered them cash which they wouldn't
 take.

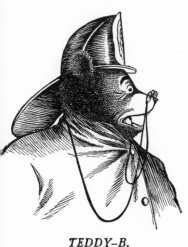

TEDDY–B.

He ordered a carriage with coachman swell,
To take them back to their hotel,
And promised to print in the local press
Their pictures large in firemen's dress.

And a full report of the fire that day
    And the things he heard the towns-folk say
        About bravery shown and the speed they made:
            Captain Muddy Pete and his fire brigade.

Said TEDDY–B, in their room that night,
    "One fire a day is enough to fight;
        I'm stiff and tired and burned and sore;
            I'm going to sleep a week or more,
                And read in bed and play I'm sick
                    Till I get tired of doing the trick."

Said TEDDY–G, as he put out the light,
"You fought one fire; I had two to fight;
But I'd rather play with a house afire
Than fool again with an electric wire."

        But long before they went to sleep
            They outlined plans next day to keep:
                The Hippodrome and the Wax Musee
                    Were things they surely had to see.

The Roosevelt Bears
see the
WAX MUSEE

The Roosevelt Bears see the WAX MUSEE

At eight o'clock the following day
The postman left, the bell boys say,
A hundred letters for each Roosevelt Bear,
From East and West and everywhere:
Letters from friends at their mountain glen
Telling of trouble with hunting men.

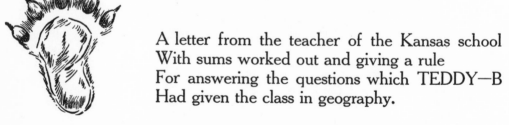

A letter from the teacher of the Kansas school
With sums worked out and giving a rule
For answering the questions which TEDDY—B
Had given the class in geography.

A letter from the farmer where they spent a day
Asking them sure to return that way.
It said that the bull which scared them blue
Would be tied by the nose when they came through.
A lawyer wrote demanding cash
For the old balloon that went to smash.

"A hundred letters for each Roosevelt Bear, from East and West and everywhere."

A Niagara lad sent local news
    And an envelope filled with Niagara views.
      A sophomore wrote to TEDDY–G
        To ask how he liked his L-D degree.

        Priscilla Alden sent a little note
          Which said she was glad their little boat
            Carried them through the storm so nice
              And landed them safe on the berg of ice.

"But TEDDY–G went straight ahead, while the machine by TEDDY–B was fed."

Letters in dozens from girls and boys
  Sending them books and candy and toys
    To give away when they wanted to treat
      Deserving lads like Muddy Pete.

The last letter opened by TEDDY–B
Was an invitation to the Wax Musee,
To visit the show that day at three.

  "I'll hire a machine," said TEDDY–G,
    "And answer my mail by electricity.
      There's one at work on the floor below,
        Where you feed in letters and let it go.

I've seen the writing of this machine,
  Like a printed page in blue and green;
    And the girl who owns it said that she
      Would give a typewriting lesson free."

"'Good afternoon,' said TEDDY–B,
'Is this Buster Brown and Tige I see?'"

Said TEDDY–B, " I'm afraid your wrong,
But if you want to try I'll go along."
So down they went to try their luck
At printing letters like a book.

The girl was out; the machine was there;
TEDDY–G sat down on the little chair
And started in with all his might
To pound the keys and make them write;
While TEDDY–B at every call
Fed in a letter, envelope and all.

"This machine writes Greek," said TEDDY–B,
As he picked up the letters the type to see;
"At least the language is new to me:
Chicago is spelled without a C,
And Boston has neither S nor T;

And Priscilla Alden would make you sick,
She's like a problem in arithmetic;
And that Kansas teacher is doing some tricks
With question marks and the figure 6;

And that farmer man, no one will blame
If he shoots us both when he sees his name.
You wrote this lawyer about the old balloon
In dollar signs enough to buy the moon."

But TEDDY–G went straight ahead
While the machine by TEDDY–B was fed
Until every letter that both Bears had
Was answered some way, good or bad.

'Twas three o'clock when they left to see
The mysteries of the Wax Musee.

They found Buster Brown in the entrance hall
And a cat climbing up the building wall
With Tige below looking up at puss
And Buster's mother trying to stop the fuss.
   "Good afternoon," said TEDDY–B,
     "Is this Buster Brown and Tige I see?"
       (Tige gave Buster a knowing wink
         Which put him wise and made him think.)

      "The Roosevelt Bears! I've heard of you;
      TEDDY–B and G! How do you do!
      You're the jolliest bears I ever saw."
         And Buster shook each by the paw
         While Tige seemed glad that he was near
         And put on a smile from ear to ear.

"You come with us," said Buster Brown,
"We know this place, upstairs and down;
There are people here in smiles and tears
Who haven't changed for a hundred years.
We'll make those laugh who look so sad
And the merry ones we'll make them mad."

      But Buster's mother made him stay
      Right where he was in wax and clay;
      And Tige looked round for a place to hide
      As the Roosevelt Bears passed on inside.

They saw the eagle which stole the child
   And carried it up in the mountains wild.
     They stopped for a moment to see the King
      And to ask Madame Patti if she would sing.

They saw Emperor William in a soldier suit,
    But to all their questions he was deaf and mute;
        So TEDDY–G, to make him look gay,
            Turned the tails of his moustache the other way.

At the Roman Forum, TEDDY–B spoke out
    And asked Mark Antony what 't was all about:
        This Roman crowd and Cæsar slain
            And why they were doing the thing again.

And thus they went from place to place
    Looking at people of every race
        And crimes committed and prisoners hung
            And no complaint from any tongue.

At the lions' den TEDDY–G was wild;
A lion had killed a little child:
"I'll go right in and smash his face."
But a man who was there to guard the place

Spoke up and said, "That lion
   in there
Is not afraid of a Roosevelt
   Bear;

He's made of wax, and that
   savage look
He wears all the time like a
   picture book."

But TEDDY–G replied that he,
If he owned the place, would
   let folks see
That lions who did such things
   as they
Shouldn't live at all in wax or
   clay.

Then on they went upstairs to guess
How Ajab played his game of chess.

Said TEDDY–G, "See if you can
Play checkers with this wooden man;
And while you play I'll take off the lid
And find out where the man is hid."

"TEDDY-G looked at him from head to heels, and his side door opened to see the wheels."

Three games were played and TEDDY–B
Won every one so fast that he
Made the wooden eyes flow free with tears,
The first time in a hundred years.

TEDDY–G looked at him from head to heels,
    And his side door opened to see the wheels,
        And the man's mainspring and his wooden heart
            He examined with care and took apart,
                But he couldn't find out high or low
                    How this man of wood made the checkers go.

TEDDY–B was polite and said "Good-bye;"
    And the man got up and wiped his eye,
        And held out his hand as well 's he could,
            (It had several pieces all made of wood)
                And said, "Your playing was pretty good."

As the Bears passed out of the Wax Musee
    A paper was handed to TEDDY–G
        Which read like this in printing bold:

"Resolved, *That mothers should never scold,*
For boys are wax and scoldings stick
And impressions can't be rubbed out quick.

Resolved, *That the world was made for play,*
And that boys and bears should have their way,
When fun is needed the blues to down."

                Signed by Tige and Buster Brown.

" The four took hands to skip and sing and to dance around in a jolly ring."

The four took hands to skip and sing,
And dance around in a jolly ring.
Folks crowded near inside and out

To see what the fun was all about.
A thousand shoppers on the street
Paused as they passed the Bears to meet.

A speech was asked from TEDDY–B
As he stepped to the door the crowd to see:
    "The U. S. boys and girls are ours;
        They're made of sunshine, love and flowers,
    We're bound with them to scatter blues
        And we're here to-day to spread the news."
When TEDDY–B these things had said
    He Buster's Resolution read,
        While Tige and Buster inside the door,
            Became wax again as they were before.

The Roosevelt Bears

visit

WEST POINT

The Roosevelt Bears visit WEST POINT

The day was fine and the Bears were free
  To take a River boat to see
    The Palisades and Tarrytown
      And to view the Hudson up and down.

A request had come from a young cadet
Of West Point school, whom the Bears had met,
To dine at the West Point Army Mess,
And to see the boys in their army dress,
And to sleep on an army barracks cot,
And to try their luck at a target shot,

And to ride bare-backed in the hurdle shute,
Or to join a band with drum and flute,
Or to hear good stories of army fights
After taps are sounded to put out the lights.
So they sent a wire to the cadet to say
That they would call that very day.

"To ride bare-backed in the hurdle shute, or join a band with drum and flute."

They made the trip with but one mishap:
The wind blew off a newsboy's cap
As he walked around on the steamer deck
Calling out the news of a railway wreck
And selling his papers and chewing gum
To the crowd of tourists "going some."

TEDDY—G made a jump as he saw it
    go
And he and the cap went down
    below.
Like a diver he struck the water right
And quick as a wink was out of
    sight.

"Man's overboard," was called aloud;
And a cheer went up from the tourist
    crowd
As they saw in the water in a little
    while
The face of a bear with a pleasant
    smile.

The boat was stopped and a rope
    thrown out,
And in answer to the captain's shout
TEDDY—G called back, "The water's
    fine;
I've got the bait; pull in your line."

"Dressed and ready for hours of fun,
With cavalry horse or battery gun."

"Like a diver he struck the water right and quick as a wink was out of sight."

It didn't take them long to get
   TEDDY–G on board, all dripping wet;
     The children laughed, he looked so queer,
       With the newsboy's cap hung on his ear.
         He bowed to tourists left and right
           And said something about his appetite.
             He asked the steward to bring on some meals
               As the steamer band played "Silver Heels."

"The children laughed, he looked so queer, with the newsboy's cap hung on his ear."

At West Point landing the
    Bears were met
By a double carriage with the
    young cadet
And a cavalry mount to escort
    them round
To see the buildings on the
    ground.
They drove about for an hour
    or less,
Then went to their barrack
    rooms to dress
In soldier suits for the evening
    mess.
TEDDY–B said he'd be
    Colonel's aide
And inspect the boys on dress
    parade,
While TEDDY–G said he'd
    march or stand
As leader of the soldier band.

The parade dismissed and the supper through,
   The Bears had nothing else to do
      But to roll themselves in barrack wraps
         And to put out the lights at the sound of taps.

At reveille at six next day
They were wide awake and
   bright and gay
And dressed and ready for
   hours of fun
With cavalry horse or battery
   gun.

The boys had fun when
   TEDDY–B
Rode a cavalry horse down a
   shute to see
How to jump the walls and
   the hurdles take
Without a tumble or balk or
   break.

The horse was tricky, but the
   Bear was game
And he made him clear each
   thing that came,
Whether wall or water or
   brush or bar.
TEDDY–B would have tried
   a railway car

Or a barn or a tree or a load of hay
   Or any old thing that came in his way.
      The finest riding, the officers say,
         That was done at West Point for many a day.

TEDDY–G took his turn at soldier fun
    When he loaded and fired a battery gun.
        He charged in powder and cannon ball;
            "So simple," he said, "it's nothing at all."

He asked a cadet his hat to keep
    Till he stepped to the muzzle to take a peep
        To see if the ball was in all right,
            And if things in front were out of sight.
                What happened next no one can tell,
                    TEDDY–G was lifted in air a spell

And whirled around so quick in space
He didn't remember just what took place.
"I caught that ball, all right," said he,
When the officer questioned TEDDY-G;

"But I don't like catching balls like that;
My place I think is at the bat.
Next time you pitch don't throw so quick;
You struck me like a load of brick."

Said the officer, "For bravery shown
We'll give you a title all your own;
You can drop your Harvard L and D
And be known as Colonel TEDDY-G."

The boys got out the fife and drum
And made things all around them hum
As they marched ahead of the Roosevelt Bears
In army step down the flight of stairs

To take the ferry at half-past four
Across the river to the other shore,
Where a train was waiting to take them down
The eastern bank and back to town.

"Let us go to-morrow," said TEDDY-G,
"And a first-class game of baseball see;
That ball they pitched at West Point school
Had hardly time enough to cool;
It struck my paws so fiery hot
I thought for a minute that I was shot."

The
Roosevelt Bears
play
BASE BALL

The Roosevelt Bears play BASE BALL

The Bears were invited by Muddy Pete
To go with him to an East Side street
To visit children who never see
Either grass or field or flower or tree.
They loaded up like old Saint Nick
With bundles piled on high and thick;
Bouquets of flowers for children sick
And toys and candy for those at play,
And a hundred other things, folks say,
Who saw them on the street that day.

They went around from door to door,
    Where bears had never been before;
        Climbed flights of stairs and bumped their heads
            To cheer up lads who were sick in beds;
                Threw bouquets into windows high,
                    And picked nice toys and let them fly,
                        And candy boxes and twigs of green,
                            Wherever boys and girls were seen.

"They loaded up like old Saint Nick, with bundles piled on high and thick."

"TEDDY-B threw the monkey and made him yell,
And caught him every time he fell."

But the jolliest sport of the day began
When they met an organ-grinder man
With a monkey trained to act the clown
And pick up pennies boys throw down.
TEDDY–G asked the man if he could go
With his monkey band for an hour or so;
TEDDY–B said he the troupe would join
And see that rich folks shelled out coin.

He'd give the monkey double pay:
Five cents an hour for half-a-day.
And the organ man may go, said they,
And join some other kind of play.
"Or if you're tired," the two Bears said,
"Go home for the day and go to bed;
We'll use your organ and monkey clown
And pay you half a dollar down
And two dollars more when we are through
And return your band as good as new.

With help from Cribs and Muddy Pete
  We'll find our way from street to street."
  This bargain made, the Bears set out
    To give the children round about
      And old folks too along the street
        The funniest kind of music treat.

TEDDY–G took the crank and just for fun
Made marches dance and two-steps run,
And polkas gallop and waltzes race
And street-songs step at a lively pace.
While TEDDY–B climbed up on top
Of the music box stood on its prop
And threw the monkey and made him yell
And caught him every time he fell.

A boy got a drum for Muddy Pete,
    And Cribs danced round on two hind feet,
        And all five laughed and cheered and sang
            And made things go with slap and bang.

The crowd of children filled the square;
Five hundred boys and girls were there;
And scores of men stopped work to see
The tricks of TEDDIES–B and G
Nickels enough and quarters too
And silver dollars, not a few,

Were collected that day by the players
    four
To give a fresh-air week down by the
    shore
To boys and girls a score or more
Who had never seen the sea
    before.

The afternoon was good and hot
And the Bears sat down in a
    vacant lot
To count their cash and rest
    their feet
And eat some lunch with Muddy
    Pete.

They returned to the organ-grinder
    man
His music-box and collection can
And his monkey clown and some
    money too,
Just as he bargained they should do.

They gave the monkey an extra dime
    For working two hours over time,
        And a box of nuts as a special treat,
            The kind that monkeys like to eat.

Seven boys came over to where they sat
With bags of sand and ball and bat
And baseball gloves and masks of wire
And asked if they the Bears could hire.

"We're going to play," a lad spoke up,
"The Bowery nine for a silver cup,
And we're short two men; good players they;
But they couldn't come to the game to-day."

"And the Bowery nine," another said,
"Are bigger boys by half-a-head,
And good at bat and quick to run;
They beat us last time two to one."

"They don't play fair," said another lad,
"They count all balls both good and bad;
They claimed a foul when I made a base
And when I objected they slapped my face."

"The Bowery nine," said TEDDY–B,
"Is the kind of nine I'd like to see;
We'll join the team and run the game
And win that silver cup just the same."

"Give me some pointers," said TEDDY–G,
"This game you play is new to me."
The Bears were coached in every rule
And they both caught on like boys at school.

The Bowery boys, in a little while,
Came on the lot in baseball style.
They read off rules to the other nine
And helped lay out the diamond line.

In size, they said, among themselves,
These Roosevelt Bears are number twelves;
But the Bowery captain bet his hat
That neither Bear could pitch or bat.

"This game," he said, "is as good as won;
  We'll beat those fellows ten to one."

A Bowery boy went to the bat
    While the other eight on some lumber sat
        To watch the play and wait their turn
            And see the Bears their fingers burn.
TEDDY–B as catcher in mask and pad
    Met every ball both good and bad
        With snap and skill so sure and quick,
            He seemed to know the baseball trick;

While TEDDY–G at the pitcher's box
Put balls to bat like hammer knocks

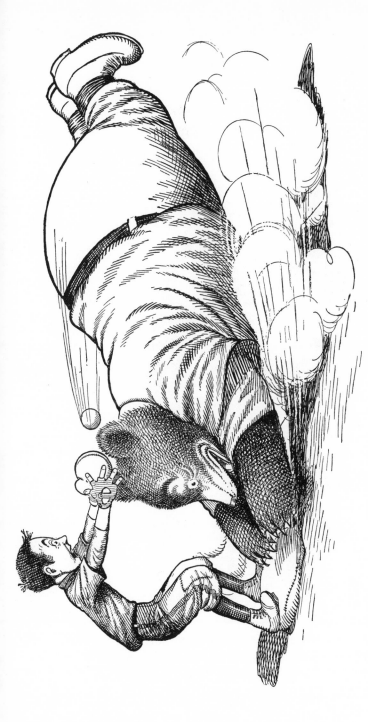

And with curves so neat and twists so new
The fielders hadn't a thing to do;
For not a boy could make a hit
And one by one the plate they quit.
Said Muddy Pete, "Their cake is dough"
As he marked the score, a great big O.
"It's our turn now," said TEDDY-B,
"We'll let those Bowery fellows see

That the team that wins this game to-day
Will make their score by honest play."
And of all the batting that was ever done
In games that lost or in games that won,
In timing hits and in making base,
And in running home in the wildest race,
This play that day of the Roosevelt Bears
Beat baseball records everywheres.

They knocked that ball so hard and high
    Above the clouds up in the sky,
        That while it tarried out of sight
            The Bears went round with all their might

And scored so fast for that silver cup
That Muddy Pete could scarce keep up.
        Nine innings each they didn't get,
        For the Roosevelt Bears would be batting yet
            If the Bowery boys hadn't stopped the score
            At naught for them to sixty-four.

The
Roosevelt Bears
arrive in
PHILADELPHIA

The Roosevelt Bears arrive in

PHILADELPHIA

The Bears went out to a country place
      To see a machine take its trial race;
            Invented by a New Jersey man
                 And made to fly on a novel plan.
This trial trip was to prove that day
That machines that fly have come to stay.
When the hour arrived to cut the cord
There wasn't a man who would go aboard.
           The Bears said they would make the trip
           And every racing record whip
           If they only knew how to steer the ship.
           "We've sailed before," said TEDDY–B,
           "We hit Chicago down a tree
           From an old balloon that brought us there
           From a Missouri town at a county fair."
              "I'm not afraid," said TEDDY–G,
              "I'd like to go to the moon to see
              If the man up there charges en-
                   trance fees
              And what he does with all the
                   cheese."

But as they talked the machine got wise
    And with buzz and whiz it began to rise
        And broke the ropes that held it tight
            And went towards the clouds and out of sight
                With TEDDY–B and TEDDY–G
                    Grabbing at anything they could see:

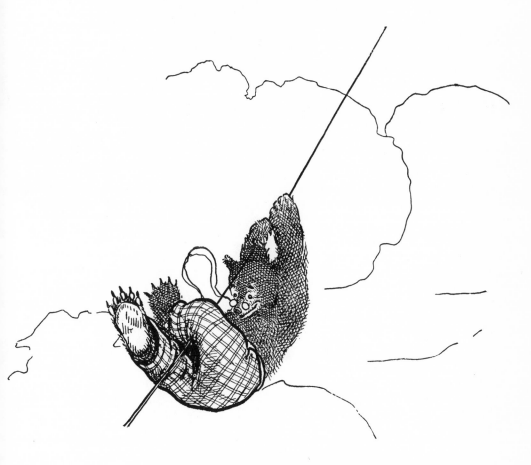

The one on a bar beneath the sail
    And the other on a rope to make a tail.
        They started so quick and went so high
            They hadn't a chance to say good-bye.

They had ridden before and lively too,
    On cow-boy horses and in frail canoe;
        In an old balloon and a 'mobile car,
            But this ride that day beat those by far.

" ' We've sailed before,' said TEDDY–B,
' We hit Chicago down a tree.' "

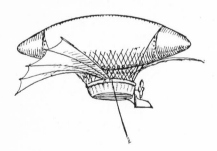 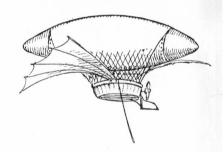

They went over town and farm and creek
In one straight line like a lightning streak,
And it wasn't forty minutes when
They came in sight of William Penn
Looking so wise and straight and tall
On the top of Philadelphia's city hall.
TEDDY–B called out from where he sat,
"There's a man ahead; I see his hat;
His hand is out; he means to try
To catch the rope as we go by."
And TEDDY–G in cow-boy style
Let out the rope, nearly half a mile,
And as it coiled he pulled with might
And William Penn he lassoed tight.
A crowd of children down below
Looked up and saw the Bears let go
And come from the clouds like sailors bold,
With not a thing but the rope to hold,

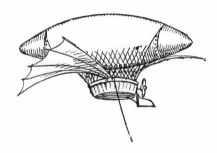 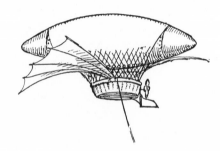

"They came from the clouds like sailors bold, with not a thing but the rope to hold."

And land all right on the old man's hat,
Where both sat down to have a chat
And look about and view the town
And ask each other how they'd get
down.

They looked over the brim to
    see Penn's face
And ask him questions about
    the place:

What would happen if they
    should fall?
And how long it took to build
    the hall?

And what it cost and if he
    thought it nice
To pay so much for expert
    advice?

And one thing sure they'd like
    to know
Why this Quaker town was
    considered slow?

A crowd soon gathered round
    the square;
Police and engineers were
    there,

And business men and children too,
    And each one wondering what to do;
        For how to get the two Bears down
           Was soon being asked by half the town.

The Mayor came out with megaphone
　　And called aloud up the tower of stone
　　　　And promised Father Penn a dime
　　　　　　If he'd give the Bears a high old time.

Not very far from where they sat
A door was opened in the Quaker hat
And a man put out his head to say
That the Roosevelt Bears could come that way,
But the door was small and it wouldn't do
For neither Bear could be crowded through.

Said TEDDY–B, "Go to the street
And bring a rope six hundred feet
And William here will hold one end
While we to the square below descend."

This plan was tried and in half an hour
The Bears had landed from the tower
And had shaken hands right then and there
With every child around the square.

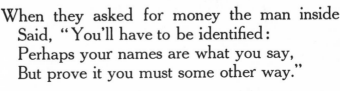

From there they went, the papers say,
To a Broad Street bank to draw their pay,
Or to cash a check which TEDDY–G
Had got in New York as their circus fee.

When they asked for money the man inside
Said, "You'll have to be identified:
Perhaps your names are what you say,
But prove it you must some other way."

"Is that check good?" said TEDDY–B,
"Well, if it is, I'll let you see
That G is he and B is me."
But before he had time to act the bear
The check was taken and the cash was there.

To a shop they went on Chestnut Street
And dressed up new from head to feet
And got the bill and paid the fee
And started out the town to see.

Two little lads named Jack and Will
Had bought four tickets for vaudeville;
Four seats up front at a children's show
That was given to help poor boys to go
To a training school where men are paid
To teach young lads a useful trade.
The boys had heard of the Roosevelt Bears
And they spent their money for the extra chairs
That very day on Chestnut Street
To give the Bears this special treat.

The boys had followed the Bears a square,
Intending to ask if they would care
To use up their time that day to go
With two little lads to the children's show.
Jack was bravest and walked close behind
To see if the Bears were really kind.
"You speak to TEDDY–B," said he,
"And I'll put the question to TEDDY–G."
"All right!" said Will, and he stepped ahead
And this to TEDDY–B he said:

"Mr. TEDDY–B, will you come with me
Right now a children's show to see?
I have your ticket; it's paid for too;
I bought it specially for you."
"That was good of you; of course I'll go,"
Said TEDDY–B, "to the children's show;
We're here to make the jolliest kind
Of fun for every child we find."
"Me too," said Jack; 'twas all he said;
His courage wasn't in his head;

"But TEDDY-G to answer Jack lifted him high up on his back."

But TEDDY–G to answer Jack
Lifted him high up on his back
And danced a jig right then and
    there

To show the crowd that a
    Roosevelt Bear
For serious people didn't care;

They lived for fun and their fun
    they'd share
Free of expense and everywhere.

But the things that happened to
    Jack and Will
That afternoon at vaudeville

Were not on the program of the
    children's show;
For the Roosevelt Bears, folks say
    who know,

Made the biggest hit of their lives
    that day
And put up an afternoon of play
The like of which was never seen
By old or young, by king or queen.

The Roosevelt Bears entertain PHILADELPHIA CHILDREN

The Roosevelt Bears entertain PHILADELPHIA CHILDREN

The theatre chairs were filled with fun,
For a boy or girl was in every one
Except the four which Jack and Will
And the Roosevelt Bears had come
    to fill.

The band was playing the latest air
And laughing children everywhere
As the Bears walked down the cen-
    tral aisle
In their summer suits cut Philadelphia
    style.

They looked so jolly and smiled so
    sweet
That the children clapped and stamped
    their feet
And waved their hands and stood on
    chairs
And cried "Hurrah for the Roosevelt
    Bears!"

But the Bears were large and the seats were small
And they found they couldn't sit down at all;
So they stood in the aisle to view the crowd,
And thus spoke TEDDY–B out loud:

"Young ladies and gentle-
        men; children dear;
And chairman too, if there
        is one here,

TEDDY–G and I have
        come to stay,
To hear you laugh and to
        see the play,

And since we can't very
        well sit down
We'll go on the stage and
        help the clown,

And stand and sit on wall or floor
        And do some tricks we have done before,
                And some quite old and some quite new,
                        And keep it up till the show is through."

The children called for
    TEDDY–G,
But he shook his head and
    said that he
Could sing a song or dance
    a jig,
Or sit on chairs either
    small or big,

Or talk to girls or with
    them dine,
But to make a speech
    wasn't quite his line.

The speeches through,
    a theatre page
Took the two Bears back
    upon the stage.

As the curtain rolled up to the top
    A man at the back asked the Bears to stop:
        "Two clowns are on the stage," said he,
            "They have started their piece and I'll let you see
            That you can't interrupt or make a noise
            Or you'll spoil this show for these girls and boys."

"Your advice is right," said TEDDY–B,
And out they went the clowns to see.
The clowns were scared when they saw the Bears
        Step up behind them unawares,
            And they ran for doors at left and right
            And as quick as wink were out of sight.

" As Dublin Mike and Pat from Cork,
They came on the stage to look for work."

But they were ordered back to earn their fee
And to take a turn with TEDDIES–B and G.
And from that hour the play went smart
For the two bears helped in every part.
They made those two clowns march and sing,
Jump over chairs and through a ring,
And climb up poles and ride a wheel
And do a clog-dance, toe and heel.
And when they finished amid loud applause
The Bears ran off on all four paws
With the clowns on backs with jolly noise
Throwing kisses back to girls and boys.
The orchestra played "A Boy called Taps"
And then appeared a troupe of Japs:
A dozen little men in tights,
The heroes of a hundred fights.

For a little while the Bears stood by
    And watched the Japs their muscles try,
        And saw them balance balls and bricks
           On parasols and billiard sticks,
                And climb up ladders out of sight
                    And fall again and land all right.
Then TEDDY–B said he'd like to do
    A Western schoolboy trick he knew.
        He made the Japs stand in a row
           And take hold of hands and not let go.
                Then he caught one end and with whirling clip
                  He showed them how to crack the whip.
The Japs went whizzing in the air
    And whirled in circles everywhere;
        But they did the trick so smart and neat
           That every Jap lit on his feet.
A man with hoops was next to play
    And he asked if TEDDY–G would stay
        And help him show the boys and girls
           How wooden hoops were taught their twirls.
                But this trick with hoops put TEDDY–G
                  In so many circles he couldn't see.

They came flying at him through the air
    And rolling in from everywhere;
        And try his best he couldn't throw
            A single hoop and make it go.

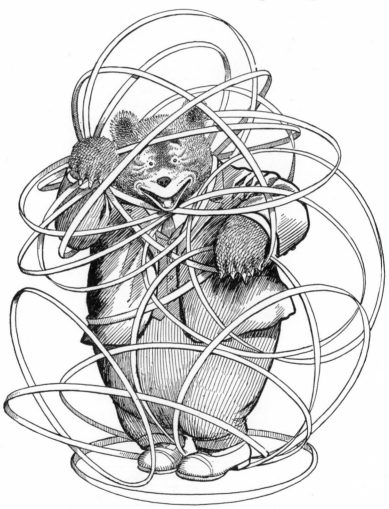

He was hooped around from head to paw,
    The funniest sight you ever saw;
        But he enjoyed the fun and said that he
            Wore rings enough that day for three.

But the jolliest thing that day was when
    The two Bears dressed as Irishmen:
        A Dublin Mike and a Pat from Cork
            Came on the stage to look for work;
                TEDDY–G as Mike with workman's hod
                    And TEDDY–B as Pat from Blarney sod;
With blackthorn sticks their foes to hit,
    And filled to the brim with Irish wit.
        Their Irish brogue in joke and song
            Made the children laugh both loud and long.

The last part of the show that day
  Was sleight of hand, the programs say,
    But why it failed to work out well
      The man who tried it couldn't tell.
                    A trunk was brought, a solid mass,
               With iron locks and bound in brass.
            The Bears were asked to get inside;
         The trunk was locked and with rope was tied

And the man announced that at his command
    He'd slide a curtain and there would stand
        The Roosevelt Bears outside and free
            With the trunk unlocked by any key.

But it didn't work; the Bears
    weren't there,
And it gave the man a little
    scare

To find he couldn't do the
    trick,
And the trunk was unlocked
    pretty quick

For fear they'd smother for
    want of air,
But the Bears had gone no one
    knows where.

The trunk was empty; not as they feared;
    The Roosevelt Bears had disappeared.
        The Bears had gone, but no one knew
            Just where to look or what to do.

Detectives hunted high and low
    And questioned folks who ought to know,
        And listened for the slightest sound
           And hunted rooms beneath the ground,
            And through the halls walked round and round,
            But not a trace of the Bears they found.

At supper-time at home that night
  The boys and girls told of their flight;
    And the jokes they cracked and tricks they played
      And the jolliest kind of fun they made.
        And how they saw them locked and tied
          So tight and fast that children cried.

Some little girls and wee boys too
  Wouldn't go to bed until they knew
    How TEDDY–B and TEDDY–G
      Got out of the trunk without a key;

          But their papas told them not to mind,
            That some one the Bears that night would find
          And the papers sure the following day
            Would explain in full how they got away.

The
Roosevelt Bears
spend a day at
ATLANTIC CITY

The Roosevelt Bears

spend a day at

ATLANTIC CITY

How the Bears got out of the box
    that day
Was never known, the children say;
But that afternoon, about half-past
    four,
They engaged fine rooms on the
    seventh floor,

About half way up and half way
    down,
Of the best hotel there was in town;
And there they stayed, enjoying a
    rest

And eating things the very best,
And seeing reporters and playing
    pool
And learning things not taught in
    school.

"There they stayed enjoying a rest, and eating things the very best."

Said TEDDY–B one morning bright,
After spending a hot and sleepless night:
"The weather's warm and sticky too
For fellows dressed like me and you;
I move we take a little run
Down to the shore for some ocean fun.

> I've heard it said that the bathing there,
> With sandy bottoms everywhere,
> Is quite a fad with men of wealth,
> Who go there simply for their health."

> > "My health is good," said TEDDY–G;
> > "And I've wealth enough for you and me;
> > But if bathing's fun, that's what I need;
> > My health consists of fun and feed."

So off they went that very day
To try Atlantic City spray

"Across the sand in running dash,
They struck the breakers with a splash."

They took a ferry to Camden town
    And got a train which shot them down
        Across New Jersey and to the sea
            So quick they scarce had time to fee

The porter boy who brushed their
    clothes
And told them that hotels in rows
Lined every street and the ocean
    front
So thick they wouldn't have to
    hunt.

And bathing houses, a score or
    more,
He said they'd find them near the
    shore.
They walked the boardwalk to
    and fro
And took a peep at every show;

They heard bands play and auctioneers
    Make speeches which reduced to tears
        The crowds of buyers who bargains sought
            But didn't need the goods they bought.

They took a turn with a wheeling chair
Of double size, to fit a bear,
With TEDDY–B, the lazy kind,
And TEDDY–G, the man behind.
A palmist read their paws to see
How long they'd live and what would be
Their fortunes in the years to come
When as millionaires they'd be going some.
They saw the fish-haul on the pier
And the loaded net with fishes queer.

They rode the donkeys on the sand
And held some children by the hand
While rides they took on donkey back
And made the bathers clear the track.

They went below with shivery feel
In a little boat where the water-wheel
Went splashing round with all its might
And pushed their boat into darkest night.

And then to a boardwalk place they went
    Two colored bathing suits to rent.
        They dressed themselves like thousands more
            Who were walking up and down the shore;
                And across the sand in running dash
                    They struck the breakers with a splash.

Of all the fun of every sort,
    Since Columbus sailed from Genoa's port,
        That the old Atlantic ever had
            With ocean bathers, good or bad,

With buccaneers or pirate crafts,
    Or shipwrecked crews on lonesome rafts,
        With fishermen in ocean wave,
            Or boats sent out their lives to save,

Or tourists bound for foreign clime
With dinners upset all the time,
With ocean fish of every form
Which swim the same in calm or storm,

With Admiral Drake or Captain Kidd
Who stole some gold and got it hid,
Or with careless boys of whom you've
    read
Who sometimes fall in over head,—

This fun the Atlantic had that day,
Some fifty thousand bathers say,
Beat every record for a thousand years
And made waves laugh themselves to
    tears.

For the Roosevelt Bears had nerve and pluck
  And as they faced each wave to duck
    They plunged right in and got upset
      Head over paws and awful wet.

They took boys out in water deep
And made them from their shoulders
    leap;
And rescued swimmers, four or five,
And brought them back to shore alive;
And when they tired of the ocean's
    whirls
They played on the sand with boys and
    girls,
And ran and danced and had lots of
    fun,
And dried themselves in the mid-day
    sun.

When back they went to get their suits,
To put on trousers, coats and boots,
Said TEDDY–G from his little house,
"This bathing suit wouldn't fit a mouse;
It's shrunk all up like a lady's glove
And won't come off by pull or shove."

Said TEDDY–B from the box next door,
"Why didn't you put on three or four?"
But TEDDY–G didn't see the joke
And said he'd rip the thing or choke.

And rip he did from end to end
In a way no stitch would ever mend.
"It came off that way both smooth and nice,"
Said TEDDY–G when he asked the price.

They went that night by lucky chance
To an ocean pier where a cake-walk dance
Was on in style with couples six
Who knew full well the cake-walk tricks.

"All four danced with toe and paw the smartest cake-walk you ever saw."

Two pickaninnies won the prize;
They beat all records for their size;
And as they did their last encore
The Roosevelt Bears went on the floor,
And all four danced with toe and paw
The smartest cake-walk you ever saw.

The dancing finished with laugh and cheer
Then all the children on the pier
Shook hands with TEDDIES–B and G
And asked them both to come to see
A children's dance, a pretty sight,
Which they would give the following night.

But the Bears replied with much regret
That Philadelphia they had not seen yet;
They must go back and crackers buy
To celebrate Fourth of July,
For they were bound to show the world
That when stars and stripes were first unfurled

And liberty rang sweet and loud
For warriors brave and patriots proud,
This flag and bell, right then and there,
Meant freedom for both man and bear.

The Roosevelt Bears celebrate the FOURTH

The Roosevelt Bears celebrate the FOURTH

TEDDY–G went out the night before
To Market Street, to a fireworks' store,
And bought a load of crackers red,
And torpedoes round like balls of lead,
And great big whirlers which you light
And then run off with all your might,
And flags and kites and pistol toys:
The kind to give to little boys;
And rockets which go whizzing high
To shoot bright stars around the sky;
And sticks to hold and turn about
While balls of fire come popping out;
And drums to beat and horns to blow,
And things to shoot and things to
     throw;
And small balloons in colors gay
And a hundred flags to give away;
In all about twelve dollars' worth
To celebrate July the Fourth.

They didn't sleep a wink that night
But started out before 'twas light,
To historic Independence Square.
"For that," said TEDDY–B, "is where
This western world beyond the sea
Unfurled the flag of liberty;
And that's the place and this the date
Where loyalty must celebrate."
"Oh you come off," said TEDDY–G,
    "It's fun that I am here to see;
        Who cares to-day who won the game?

TEDDY–G—His paw

We'll shoot off crackers just the same."
And this is how the two Bears talked
As down the street to the Square they walked:

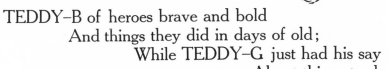

TEDDY–B of heroes brave and bold
    And things they did in days of old;
        While TEDDY–G just had his say
            About things to do that very day.

At the Liberty Bell they took a try
And hoisted it up good and high
And rang it out both loud and clear,
And at every ring there went up a cheer;
For the only day in all the year
When the crack doesn't spoil the tone sent forth
Is Independence Day, July the Fourth.
TEDDY–B—His paw   At least that's what the children say,
And they know this bell from Z to A.

But the fun began with the Roosevelt Bears
When boys stole on them unawares
And put a match to TEDDY–G
　　　In his coat-tail pocket, where, you see,
　　　He had stored some crackers, a good-sized bunch,
　　　Along with hard-boiled eggs for lunch.

" At the Liberty Bell they took a try,
And hoisted it up both good and high."

Lickety-split-pat-pit-bang-boo!
 And the coat tail smoked and split in two,
  And hard-boiled eggs shot here and there
   And the Bear went up and down in air.
    But he told the lads he didn't care,
     That fun might start in anywhere;

At front or back, in hat or boot,
 Put punk to powder and let it shoot.
  "We are out," he said, "for fun and noise
   And when fun is trump, boys will be boys."
    And from that hour the lads and he
     Shared all there was to do or see.

They strung a wire from tree
 to tree,
And then the fellows with
 TEDDY–B
Put crackers all along the
 wire,
To prepare the field for an
 army fire.

Said TEDDY–G, as he
 explained the play,
"We'll fasten a flag on the
 wire half-way,
And you boys under yonder
 tree
Who have taken sides with
 TEDDY–B,

When I say the word, you
 put your fire
At the cracker next you on
 the wire,

"They strung a wire from tree to tree and then the fellows with TEDDY-B
Put crackers all along the wire, to prepare the field for an army fire."

While I, if my boys a hand will lend,
Will put a match to the other end.
To reach the flag first, that's the game,
And the side which wins this piece of fame
Wins all the crackers big or small
Which haven't gone off when time I call.

If on both sides the armies flunk
Both captains use again their punk."
When both the sides the rules did know
TEDDY–G called out, "One! two! three! Go!"

And at the words two armies
shot
Their cracker guns both
quick and hot
As on they marched along
the wire
In powder smoke and blaz-
ing fire.

The flag was won by
TEDDY–G
And prisoners taken, ninety-
three
Of the finest crackers the
others had,
All not shot off, both good
and bad.

But this army game was children's play
    Compared with things they did that day:
        From noon till night they let things go,
            In sky above and on earth below,

With slap and bang, in smoke and noise,
  Like any two July Fourth boys.

They sent balloons up to the clouds
  And a dozen kites to please the crowds,
    And then shot rockets just to try
      To hit the things up in the sky;

They dug a hole down in the ground
    And filled it full of crackers round
        And shot them off to hear the sound.

           They burned their paws and scorched their hair,
        And when darkness came they did their share
     Of firing rockets everywhere,
   And in burning lights, a fiery red,
Till long past time for going to bed.

When the day was o'er said TEDDY–B,
"Let's go to-morrow to the Zoo to see
The animals imprisoned there:
The elephant and polar bear,
The lions, tigers, and kangaroos,
And tell them one and all the news:

That July the Fourth is the day that we
Who own and love this country
Do celebrate in smoke and noise,
That we may teach our girls and boys
That this one day of every year
Is given them free to shout and cheer,

As a safety valve for them and you
　　To keep things running square and true."

Said TEDDY–G, "I'll freedom teach
   And try to practise what I preach;
      To-morrow I'll let out the Zoo,
         The elephants and monkeys too,
            And the polar bear and kangaroo;
               They're just as good as me or you."

The Roosevelt Bears visit the ZOO

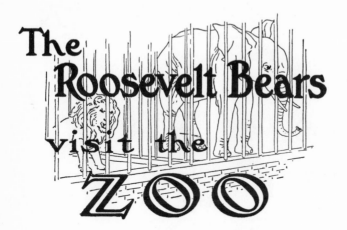

The Roosevelt Bears visit the ZOO

Said TEDDY–G, "The thing to do,"
  As they reached the high fence round the Zoo,
    In the early morning, about half-past two,
    "Is to get in there with this load of cake
    Before the keepers are wide awake."
    "You climb the fence," said TEDDY–B,
    "And throw this rope back here to me,
    And pull up the baskets one by one
      And we'll land in there a good-sized ton
      Of the finest cake that was ever made,
      And strawberry tarts and lemonade
      And cherry pie and sugar sticks
      And red ice cream in good-sized bricks
      And peanut candy and chocolate eclairs
    And other things quite new to bears."

"Don't waste your time in telling me;
I bought these things," said TEDDY–G;
And up he climbed, with business sense,
A tree which grew beside the fence,

And out a limb and dropped below
And called out, "All right; I'm in; let go."
And up went baskets two by two
Over the fence into the Zoo;

And before the day began to break
   The Bears had camped with their load of cake
      On a grassy knoll where they couldn't hide
         And with dens and pens on every side.
           "We're in here now," said TEDDY–B;
             "What do you say we do?" said he.
"Let's feed the animals," said TEDDY–G;
   "I move we let out two or three
      And bring them here and feed them cake
         And see just how our show will take;
           And if they are pleased, why we'll go round
             And let loose everything on the ground."
To the elephant house the two Bears went
   And stirred up the biggest elephant,
      And marched him over to their cake
         Before he had time to get half awake.
"You mind these things," said TEDDY–G,
"Our breakfast hour is half-past three.
   If you are good you can have a snack
      To keep you chewing till we come back."
         And they gave old Bolivar (that was his name)
           Some things to eat till back they came.

"' You mind these things,' said TEDDY–G,
' Our breakfast hour is half-past three.'"

Then off they went to the monkey cage
Where monkeys of every size and age
Were using hands and feet and lungs
And saying good-morning in a thousand tongues.

TEDDY–B made them promise they'd be good
(At least that's what he understood)
If he'd open the cage and let them out
And give them an hour to run about.

"We have," said he, "some pie and cake
Which TEDDY–G will undertake
To serve out free in an hour or two
To every animal in the Zoo.

We'll give you as much as
you deserve
If you'll act as waiters and
help us serve."
The monkeys grinned
from ear to ear
And winked at each other
a little queer,
And nodded their heads
and seemed to say
That the two Bears' orders
they'd obey.

The cage was opened and
the crowd went out,
Little and big, with laugh
and shout,
Upsetting each other
across the green,
The funniest bunch that
was ever seen.

The Bears went
then to the
beaver pond

And told the
beavers if they
were fond

Of good ice
cream served
by baboons

To bring on their
tails to use for
spoons.

They saw some foxes red and gray
And asked them to dine with them
    that day.
The wolves looked hungry and said
    they'd see
That all left over was given them
    free.

The rhinoceros couldn't accept their treat;
He had some rheumatics in his feet.
But in a cage near-by a kangaroo
Jumped twenty feet when they let him through.

An ostrich standing six feet high
        Called out to the Bears as they went by
                To hurry around with a piece of pie.

Two mountain goats with
    curling horn
Said the mountain crest where
    they were born,

Their father rented just for
    thanks
To the Roosevelt Bears to play
    their pranks,

And this they thought was
    cause indeed
Why they should be asked to
    the morning feed.

A hedgehog and a porcupine
Were the next pair asked by
    the Bears to dine,
Then a dromedary chewing
    his cud
Said he wouldn't budge from
    where he stood,

But if they'd bring him a piece
    of cake
He'd see if he liked their kind
    of bake.

From there they went to the animals' cage
    Where they found the tigers in a rage
        And the lions roaring to beat the band
            In language the Bears didn't understand.

A chimpanzee came
    near to see
And he made a face at
    TEDDY–G.
He was eating pie and
    said he feared
That their basket lunch
    had disappeared.

The Bears took warning
    and started back
To find ten keepers on
    their track,
    And animals both
        big and small
Running wild on
    every mall,
And Bolivar with his
    trumpet loud
Calling for help to
    stop the crowd.

The monkeys had gone in a solid bunch
    And captured the whole of the picnic lunch,
        And out on limbs and high up on poles,
            And on top of roofs and into holes,
                And every monkey with cake or jam,
                    Or pie or tart or sandwich ham,

Or nuts or lemonade or cheese;
    And Bolivar shaking poles and trees,
        And hungry wolves and the kangaroo,
            And mountain goats and a deer or two
                Running wild from place to place,
                    Helping on the monkey chase.

"The monkeys had gone in a solid bunch and captured the whole of the picnic lunch."

'Twas noon that day when keepers ten
    And a police brigade of fifty men,
        And a hundred boys and firemen six
            Got the monkey troupe to stop their tricks.

The Bears looked on throughout the show
    And helped on the fun by laughing so
        For TEDDY–G, since he was a cub,
            Or at Bunker Hill down in the Hub,
                Said that making fun seemed to be his forte
                    And that he never had such lively sport.

But the keeper made him change his laugh
    When he locked them up with a big giraffe
        And told them to stay and pay a fine
            When the police court met next day at nine.

The Roosevelt Bears go FISHING

The Roosevelt Bears go FISHING

When the Roosevelt Bears had paid
  their fine
For the mischief done and the monkey
  shine,
They said good-bye to the big giraffe
And told him his neck was too long by
  half;

And asked the time it took his food
  To reach his body from where he chewed;
    And why he held his head so high,
      And the size of collars he had to buy;

And why he was neither round nor square;
  But the old giraffe didn't seem to care;
    He wagged his tail and winked his eye
      And nodded his head to say good-bye.

When they quit the Zoo and got outside,
  "Let us take a train for a little ride;
    I'm tired of town and want to see
      A farm or stream," said TEDDY–B.

So a train they took without the fare,
    For where it went they didn't care.
        When "Tickets, please," the conductor said,
            TEDDY–G began to scratch his head
                And to think up names of towns he knew,
                    Like Hoboken and Kalamazoo;

But when "Tickets, please," he said again,
    TEDDY–G got busy with a ten
        And said, "Take this for your railway pay
            And stop the train some time to-day
                Where fishing's good if you go that way."
                    The conductor asked them questions strange
                      About their plans as he gave them change

And slips of paper with holes
   punched through;
He said a fishing stream he
   knew;

He'd stop the train at any rate
And show them where to buy
   some bait
And fishing poles and hook and
   line
And a jolly inn to sleep and
   dine.

They reached the place that day
   at two,
And said good-bye to the
   railroad crew,

"They met a lad on his way from school,
  Whom they stopped to question about a rule."

And went by a path up a mountain ridge
    As the train went on across a bridge.
        They found the place and got fitted out
            With six poles apiece both long and stout,
                And bait enough and lines and hooks
                    To fish a year in a dozen brooks.
For said TEDDY–G, " If fishing's play
Then I want enough, for I mean to stay
Right by the game for at least a week
Until every fish that's in the creek
Is caught and cleaned and cooked and ate
Or cut up in pieces to use for bait."
So down their rods and lines they took
To the stream below to try their luck.

                  Of all the fishing that
                      was ever done
                  By Izaak Walton or his
                    eldest son,
        Or by boys who fish with pins for hooks,
        That we read about in the picture books,
    Or for salmon trout which weigh a ton
    That they say are caught in Oregon,

Or for shad in the River
    Delaware,
Or for pike or black bass
    anywhere,
The fish that day caught by the
    Bears
Would take first prizes at all the
    fairs;

And the way they caught them
    left and right,
And the way they coaxed the
    fish to bite,
And the way they tossed the
    fish in air,
Landing in trees and everywhere,
And the way they made the
    chipmunks run,
The fish, themselves, enjoyed
    the fun.

For one fish spoke, vows
    TEDDY–G,
A great big pounder, two or
    three,
And said he wouldn't miss the
    game
Even if he never lived again.
"A sport," he said, "like
    TEDDY–G,
Is the kind that fishes love to
    see."

TEDDY–G got his line caught in a tree
And climbed up on high to get it free
When a 'possum called down from above,
"If you come up here you'll get a shove
Which will toss you off and break your head
And put you fifteen weeks in bed."
But TEDDY–G just shook with glee
And said, "I'll come right up to see."
The 'possum scared and trembled so
He fell off the limb and down below
Where TEDDY–B broke an ugly fall
By catching him like a rubber ball.
They fed that 'possum fishes eight
And gave him hook and line and bait
And told him stories about the Zoo
And the things they let the monkeys do.

They met a man by the stream that day
Who has fished for a hundred years they say,
In ocean, river, creek and pond,
And mountain brook and lake beyond,
With statesmen bold and actors gay,
And farmer lads found by the way.

He told them stories of fish he'd caught,
And when fish were few, of fish he'd bought.
And then had talked of this big land
And of men he knew on every hand:
The true to love and those to hate
Who fish for gain with stolen bait.

He told them how to have most fun
When they struck the town of Washington;
"Because," he said, "though I'm on the shelf,
I had some fun there once myself."

TEDDY–B said he would like to know
How near a Roosevelt Bear could go
To the Capitol or Monument
Without being shot by the President.

But the man replied, "Trout-
fishing's fine,
But shooting bears isn't in my
line.

Take my advice and take your
gun
When you turn your steps
towards Washington."

They shook his hand both
long and tight
And said they'd leave that
very night.

They could get a train, they
said, at four
For Washington and Baltimore.

They tramped along a country pike
And wished for horses, train or bike,
Till they met a lad on his way from school,
Whom they stopped to question about a rule
To multiply and square and add,
And what teachers did with lessons bad,
And who made spelling and what 'twas for,
And the day and hour of the next big war,
And what athletics were all about,
And where figures go when you rub them
    out,
And why the moon isn't always round,
And the difference between a noise and
    sound,
And on a fence, how long 'twould take
To rest an hour or a dinner bake,
And how things inside the earth were done,
But the lad couldn't answer a single one.

Said TEDDY-G: " If it doesn't rain,
    And you'll tell us where to get a train
        And the fare to pay and how long the run
            From the place you name to Washington,

And your age and weight and greatest height,
    And two bears you know that never bite,
        I'll give you a dollar, quick as wink,
            And let you have it before you think."

Though he never learned this dollar
    trick
The lad was bright and he answered
    quick,
And they said good-bye and it didn't
    rain
Till they stepped on board their Pullman
    train.

Said TEDDY–G, as he lit his pipe,
And bought some apples red and ripe,
And settled down in an easy seat
With a resting-place for both his feet,
" I'm tired of clothes; I'm tired of fun;
When I see the town of Washington
I'm off again for the woolly West;
I like the mountains much the best;
I want to live as free as air;
I'm satisfied to be a bear."

"But you forget," said TEDDY-B,
　　"That all these things we came East to see
　　　　Were made by the brains of every clime
　　　　　　To keep folks working all the time."

"That's all right," said TEDDY-G,
"They can work ahead, but as for me
I don't believe that bears were made
To be busy always at a trade."

The Roosevelt Bears in PITTSBURG

The Roosevelt Bears in PITTSBURG

They were on the train and at their ease
When the conductor called out "Tickets, please."
"We have no tickets," said TEDDY–G,
"But cash we have, as you will see,
And to Washington we want to go
  To see the President and to let him know
  That we are fully satisfied
  That Uncle Sam is tall and wide
  And big around, of mighty girth,
  The greatest show on all the earth;
  His boys and girls are full of fun
  From Omaha to Washington."

But the conductor said, "You ought to know
If to Washington you want to go
You've started wrong; this train you're on
Is a Pittsburg special from Washington;
  And to-morrow morning, if we're not late,
    You'll be in Pittsburg at half-past eight."

The Bears looked dazed and then
    looked mad,
And then they laughed and both
    looked glad.

Said TEDDY–B, "Pay
    up the fares;
We'll pass to-morrow
    as millionaires
And found a library
    and put through
    a deal
Of high finance in
    oil or steel."

But TEDDY–G didn't
    think so far;
He thought of night
    and the sleeping
    car;

He recalled some cranky things he said
    When they made him sleep in an upper bed
        On a train out West, and the banjo song,
            And the things they did a little wrong
                Till both were put right off the train
                    On a Kansas farm in a shower of rain.

The conductor heard this wise remark:
    "If on this train, when the night is dark,
        You want this Bear to behave himself,
            Don't make him sleep on a Pullman shelf."

But the trip was made
   without mishap
And both the Bears
   enjoyed a nap
In lower berths till eight
   o'clock,
When the porter gave
   their berths a knock
And said, "Get up; it's
   broad day light;
The Iron City is now in
   sight."

But things outside looked
   black as night
And said TEDDY–B,
   "Do you mean to
   say
That this is Pittsburg
   and this is day?"

The man replied, "Get up; that's smoke;
Take my advice and when you joke
About this town, don't do it loud,
   For Pittsburg people live in a cloud,
   And their ideas about a bear
   May be colored some by Pittsburg air."
      "What's that you say?" called TEDDY–G,
      "You seem to know your geography,
      But let me say right here and now,
      I'll teach your Pittsburg people how
To dance and sing, to laugh and joke,
   In mountain air or city smoke,
      For they must know this very day
      That Pittsburg too was made for play."

"Said TEDDY-B, ' Pay up the fares,
We'll pass to-morrow as millionaires.' "

They took a cab to a big hotel
  Where things are done both smart and swell;
    And breakfast over, TEDDY-B

On mischief bent, went out to see
  What the telegraph and phone could do
    To get a crowd their tricks to view.

He called up schools, every one in town,
And ordered all the children down
To the Old Block House at noon to see
The Teddy Bears teach history.

Then on the Mayor he played a lark
By ordering the police to Schenley Park,
To be locked up there till after dark;
"For," said TEDDY–B, "the police you know
Might spoil our little Block House show."

At costume shops each Teddy Bear
Bought a lot of Indian things to wear.
They planned at the Old Block House to meet
At the corner of a nearby street,
                    And from that spot like Indians race
                    And take possession of the place.
                    They did the trick in Wild West style;
                    Their whoops and yells were heard a mile;

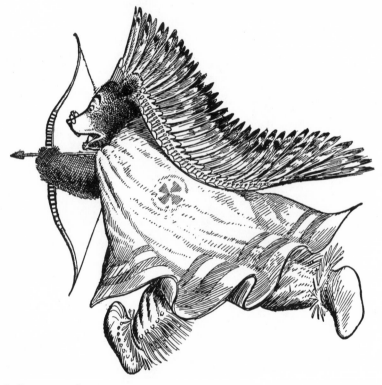

But the fight was short; no one to scare;
There wasn't a soul there anywhere.
They made the place from roof to floor
                    Like seventeen hundred and sixty-four
                    And put things into shape to fool
                    The boys and girls from every school.

The children came,
five thousand
strong,
A happy, merry,
lively throng;

The little ones by
teachers led
To study history,
they said,

But the history les-
son learned that
day
Was livelier stuff,
the fellows say,

Than most boys learn at public school;
For it didn't follow any rule,
But just shot off with laughter loud
In every corner of the crowd.

The Teddy Bears, as Indians brave,
Did everything but behave:
They chased each other round the Block
With bow and arrow and tomahawk;

"They chased each other round the Block with bow and arrow and tomahawk."

They climbed to the roof and danced a jig
  And called to children small and big
    To catch the arrows every time
      And bring them back and get a dime;
        And then to finish up the sport
          They asked the boys to take the fort:
            The boys to be the soldiers bold
              And they as Indians the place to hold.

In this the boys came out ahead;
  The Bears pretended they were dead,
    While the boys to do the thing up well
      Sent two dead Bears to the hotel.
        In half an hour they lived again
          And were out on bicycles for a spin;

This time to see men making
 steel,
And in Highland Park to have
 a wheel,
And to see the Zoo and the
 Bridge of Sighs,
And Luna Park, where they
 won the prize.

In the afternoon they put up a
 lark
At the entrance gate of High-
 land Park.
A little lad who flew a kite
Had got the string caught
 good and tight
On the entrance post when
 TEDDY–G
Climbed up the post and said
 that he
Would untie the knot and start
 the kite
Up to the sky and out of sight.

A rope was lying twirled
 around
Where workmen left it on the
 ground,
And TEDDY–G as quick as
 wink
And before the men had time
 to think

Caught up the rope and made it tight
    From post to post, from left to right,
        And out he went like a circus clown
            And whirled around, head up and down,
                And walked the rope and made more play
                    Than folks had seen for many a day.

At six o'clock they said good-bye
      To busy streets and smoky sky
            And to boys and girls for the day of fun
                  And started back towards Washington.

Said TEDDY–B, as a town they passed
      Where furnaces made fiery blast,
            "I'd rather be a Teddy Bear
                  Than stand that heat and work in there;
                  But this old world was made, they say,
                  So that men would work and bears could play."

The
Roosevelt Bears
get out a
NEWSPAPER

The Roosevelt Bears get out a NEWSPAPER

When the station clock was striking four
The Bears got off at Baltimore.
They met a newsboy on the street
Who said the newsboys were to meet
That night at six in a nook of theirs
And they'd like to have the Teddy Bears
Drop in and help them plan and think
How best to earn some extra chink.
Said TEDDY–B, "I'd like to walk
Around to your club and hear you talk
And make a speech and help along
With dance or story, trick or song."
"You ought to know," the lad replied,
"That some months ago a newsboy died.
That night his papers didn't sell
And he had no home; no one to tell
How cold he was and hungry too,
And he just died; was frozen through.
We mean to give a newsboys' show
To buy a home where the boys can go."

"They met a newsboy on the street who said the newsboys were to meet that night at six in a nook of theirs."

This story stirred up TEDDY–G,
"You leave that show to me," said he,
"I'll use my wit from nose to paw
To make more cash than you ever saw."
"I have a plan," said TEDDY–B,
"Let us run a paper just to see
If our sheet won't sell like sixty-three.

> We'll fill each page with jolly stuff
> And give the boys the greatest puff.
> We'll raise the price and earn the pay
> To build that home in half a day."

So off they went to try their hand
At a job they didn't understand:
To edit, proof-read, print and sell
A newspaper and do it well.

The publisher took them all about
To show how a paper is gotten out.
They questioned every man they met
And with the manager made a bet
That they could put each page in rhyme
And get the paper out on time.
The bet was taken; the job was theirs;
A paper run by Teddy Bears
And they to have their own sweet way
With news and ads for a single day.
They said they'd do the best they could
And make a sheet that was bright and good.

Of all the orders boys ever hear
    Who work on papers all the year,
        The orders given to the boys that night
            Beat every record out of sight.
                They made the editors fume and frown,
                    And reporters chase all around the town,

And telegraph instruments click in chime,
And telephone bells ring all the time,
And linotypes go double speed
And set up type big enough to read,

And advertisers fight for space,
    And presses go at double pace,
        And everything hum on every floor
            To beat all "scoops" ever made before.

But the paper was out on time next day:
The greatest paper, newsboys say,
That was ever printed in all the land
By the fastest press or done by hand.

"When Teddy Bears would rulers be,
And hunt for men in cave or tree."

They had floods and fires, and earthquakes, too;
And kings beheaded and discoveries new,
And ships upset and railroad wrecks,
And ten millionaires break their necks;
And the sun eclipsed at twelve at night,
And Japan start up another fight;
And Russia move clean off the earth,
And an elephant sleep in an upper berth;
And Niagara Falls turn upside down,
And the President wear a golden crown;
And ten feet of snow right in July,
And a man discovered nineteen feet high;
And robberies eight and murders ten,
And mosquitoes kill ten thousand men;
And a Wall Street smash, the worst in years,
That made the bulls and bears shed tears;

And Robinson Crusoe come back to life
And land in Baltimore with a wife;
And little Bo Peep who lost her sheep
Sold at auction mighty cheap;
And the money hid by Captain Kidd
Found in a box without a lid
By a colored boy in the Isle of Wight
A hundred thousand dollars bright.
A diamond mine they said was found
On Charles Street above the ground,
They had boys at school their lessons know,
In headlines deep a foot or so;
And all the girls in the world combine,
To go to bed at half-past nine,
Or if rules they broke to pay a fine.
And ending up on the final page
A prophecy of a future age

When Teddy Bears would rulers be
And hunt for men in cave or tree
With guide and gun, with horse and hound,
In a Colorado hunting ground.
The advertisements made that night
Were what the printers call a fright:
All shoved together, old and new,
  Upside down and wrong side too,
    Grocers had hats and caps for sale,
    And tailors eggs, and barbers ale,
    And department stores had railroad ads,
    And big hotels sold writing pads,
  And music stores sold soap and tea,
  And theatres said admission free,
  And a jeweller, the best in town,
  Offered cheap a wedding gown.
A private school sold cheese and lard,
And furniture was offered by the yard.
When TEDDY–B saw what was done
He said he thought 'twould make good fun.
"For we mean," said he, "to sell our sheet
And every record sale to beat."

The papers sold at first for ten,
But when approved by business men
The price went up on every hand;
And with papers in such brisk demand
You couldn't get a single sheet
By ten o'clock upon the street.
  The money made for the boys that day
    Bought them a home with grounds to play
    And enough to spare to give each lad
      The jolliest time he ever had:
        A fresh air week down by the sea
          With candy, cake and soda free.

The Bears were glad when their work was done
    To start for the town of Washington,
        To see the President and shake his hand
            And then go home, as they had planned.

The Roosevelt Bears
visit
WASHINGTON
and complete their
Tour of the East

The Roosevelt Bears visit WASHINGTON
and complete their Tour of the East

When the Bears arrived in Washington
    They set out at once to buy a gun.
        They bought three guns and pistols ten
           And suits and belts like fighting men.
                When dressed complete then off they went
                    To the house where lives the President.
When they reached the grounds and the
      entrance gate
No one was near to make them wait.
The news had spread round everywheres
Of this visit planned by the Roosevelt
      Bears.
A policeman dodged behind a tree
When he got first sight of TEDDY–B.
Detectives wise with eagle eye
Didn't stop to ask the reason why,
But ducked their heads behind a wall
And got under cover one and all.
A doorkeeper in gold and black
Said, "Wait a minute till I come back."

"Dee-lighted."

And lawyers bold and statesmen brave
  Who make the President behave
    Moved out of sight as quick as wink;
      To offer help they didn't think;
        But they were hunters just the same,
          Though hunting bears wasn't quite their game.

The boys who answer the call of bells
   Lost all the breath they use for yells
      In crossing lawns in serious fright;
         They ran for home with all their might.

And secretaries, three or four,
Got under desks down on the floor
When they saw the Bears at the entrance door.

        But one little lad who was playing round
      When he saw the Bears, he stood his ground
    And stepped up bravely to TEDDY–G
And said, "Who is it you want to see?"

Said TEDDY–G in his kindliest way,
"We have traveled East and have come
  to-day
To see the hunter who doesn't
  scare
And who isn't afraid of man
  or bear."

The Bears by the lad were keenly eyed,
And he said as he beckoned them both
  inside:
"My Dad's in here; but wipe your feet;
I think you're the kind he likes to meet."

They stepped inside, and the man they saw
Looked them over from head to paw
And with outstretched hand and smiling face
He gave them welcome to the place.

Said TEDDY–G, when he caught his
  breath,
"I thought this call meant certain death.
We armed ourselves with loaded gun
When we struck this town of
  Washington,
For here 'twas said we'd surely see
The man who chased bears up a tree
And with both eyes shut on darkest
  night
Could hit a bear and win a fight."

"To stand your ground," said
  TEDDY–B,
"Is the thing that we Bears like to see;
If fighting's trump or simply fun,
We stand, eyes front, and never run;
But those men of yours who guard
  your fort
Should be taken West for a little sport
And taught the things you learned out
  there
When climbing mountains chasing
  bear."

But he simply laughed at what they said
And joked of stories he had read
In newspapers of things they'd done
On their journey East to Washington.

They talked away for an hour or two
Of hunting trips and friends they knew,
And this country wide and its cities great
From Boston Hub to the Golden Gate.

The Bears were asked to come next day

At an early hour to have a play

On the White House grounds and in children's tent
And to breakfast with the President.

This visit o'er they started out
To see the buildings all about:
The Capitol with its rounded dome
Where the U. S. Senate makes its home,

And congressmen from every State
Gather in halls to deliberate;
The Treasury with its vaults of gold,
As much as a dozen trains could hold,

And silver too, and crisp bank notes
  Enough to load a hundred boats;
    The Library with its pictured halls
      And books stored high within its walls;
The gardens with their trees and flowers,
  And a museum where they stayed for hours;
    And last of all, built straight and high,
      A shaft that stands against the sky,
        Set off with stones which good friends sent
          In memory of a president.

"With outstretched hand and smiling face,
He gave them welcome to the place."

TEDDY–G said he would like to see
That famous little cherry tree
And get some cherries red and sweet
To take back home to give a treat
To the big raccoon and the mountain goat
And the old cougar and the young coyote,
To make them square and help them try
To tell the truth and not to lie.

So off they went that day at three
Out in the country the farm to see
Where George's father used to stop
And where the boy learned how to chop.

They found the place as the guide books said
And the cherry stump, but no cherries red;
The stump was there and the hatchet too
And neither looking very new.

Said TEDDY–B when these things he saw
And took the hatchet in his paw:
"Of all the shrines of history
Which you and I came East to see
This spot right here I say is trump;
This hatchet and this cherry stump."

TEDDY–G said he would like to try
Little George's axe on a tree near-by,
To prove to the world that he could do
A trick like that and own up too.
And chop he did an apple tree
And left a note where all could see,
"This tree was chopped by TEDDY–G."

They breakfasted the following day
        With the President and had their play
                For an hour before, from early dawn,
                        With boys and girls upon his lawn.
                                They asked the President if he
                                Would come out West their home to see;
                                Said TEDDY–B, "We'll treat you white
                                And put you up both day and night
With grizzly bears and panthers wild
        And give you sport not quite so mild
                As driving Congress with its load,
                        Or riding horseback down the road."

"This strenuous life," said TEDDY-G,
"Is too hard work by half for me;
I'll start back home this very day
And for a month at home I'll stay
And rest my eyes and sleep and eat
And get down again on all four feet."
Said TEDDY-B, "Our journey's through;
There's nothing left to see or do.
We were treated well everywhere we went;
And we have seen the President.
And now for home, that's what I say;
But I mean to journey back this way
To take a boat for London town
To see the king and his golden crown."
The reporters called that afternoon
When they heard the Bears were going so soon
And begged a column at least of news
About their trip and plans and views.
TEDDY-B wrote out in boldest hand
These lines that all can understand:

"To the boys we say be always gay,
And with jolly play fill every day.
Be brave, be true, be square and white,
And don't forget to your friends to write.
And to the girls: We've no advice;
You're everyone both sweet and nice.
And to all the people whom we've met
Please say we leave, with much regret,
For our mountain cave and brook and tree."

Signed

As their train pulled out an army band
Played airs well known o'er all the land;
And boys and girls waved their good-byes.
And tears filled many children's eyes.
TEDDY–B called back to the crowd that he
Would come East again each one to see.
And TEDDY–G said he'd do his best
To treat them well if they came out West.

The Teddy Bears arrive home

As they crossed the country from East to West
    They stayed in their sleeping car to rest;
        And but once or twice looked out to see
            The towns passed through and country.
Said TEDDY–G, "I'd like again
To see that farm where we have been,
And that country school and those boys at play,
For that was our very jolliest day."
"What I wish most," said TEDDY–B,
"Is when we get off this train that we
Shall have those horses to carry our load
Back over the hills on the mountain road."

The horses were there with saddle and rein
And met the Bears at the railway train,
And six mountain goats like baggage men
Were there to help them to the glen.
As back they traveled that mountain road,
The goats heaped high with the baggage load,
And the Teddy Bears on broncho backs,
Piled front and back with loaded sacks,
They looked like bandits with their spoil,
Or highwaymen after a day of toil,
Or perhaps more like true knights of old
Returning home with captured gold.
As they approached the place where they were born
    TEDDY–G blew loud on a trumpet horn
        A West Point bugle call he knew,
            And a thousand friends came into view,
                The Teddy Bears to greet with cheers
                    By this animal camp of mountaineers;

"The Teddy Bears on Broncho backs piled front and back with loaded sacks."

For the news had scattered far and wide
    When the Bears would reach the mountain side,
        And the crowd had come from far and near
            To welcome back two friends so dear.

The old bobcat with the bandaged knee
Was the first to shake with TEDDY–B,
And a young cougar and a panther bold
Helped TEDDY–G his load to hold,
        And two big-horn sheep and a mountain deer
        Stood up on stumps to lead each cheer,
        And hundreds more gave welcome hand
        To the most famous bears in all the land.

They had gifts for each bought in the East
And they passed them round at the evening feast,
And then told stories for nights and days
About their trip and the city ways,
        And the fun they had and the tricks they played
        And the things they saw and where they stayed,
        And last and best, the time they spent
        In Washington with the President.

"They had gifts for each bought in the East, and they passed them round at the evening feast."

As the Bears turned in to their own home nest
　　And curled up snug for the winter's rest,
　　　　Said TEDDY-G, as he fell asleep,
　　　　　　"If I should pray for things to keep
　　　　　　　　Of what I've seen either East or West,
　　　　　　　　　　Its boys and girls I like the best."